THE MIRRORED ROOM

ANTHONY CROWLEY

ISBN: 1482789957
ISBN-13: 978-1482789959

DEDICATION

I dedicate this work to the genius of what life represents and to the creative Artists of the past & present for shining an eternal light in us all

CONTENTS

Acknowledgments

Chapter One   1

Chapter Two   5

Chapter Three   7

Chapter Four   12

Chapter Five   17

Chapter Six   22

Chapter Seven   26

Chapter Eight   29

Chapter Nine   34

Chapter Ten   37

CONTENTS

Chapter Eleven   42

The Gathering   52

About the author   61

bibliography   63

Future works   67

ACKNOWLEDGMENTS

I would like to thank Steve Emmett, Julia Kavan & the Massacre publishing Team, (HWA) Horror Writers Association, Catherine Cavendish, James Chambers, Lauren Carroll, David Coverdale & 'Whitesnake' Barry Skelhorn at Sanitarium magazine & Eye Trauma Press, Gloria Estefan, Sophi Alvarez, Magento Nero, Spectral Press, John F.D.Taff, Julie Brown & Eatsleepwrite, Asylumink.net, Darkness beckons, HelloHorror' magazine, Jason & Book & Lantern Publishers, Neko Lily & Brutal Books, Oscar & promotehorror.com, horrornovelreviews.com, Emily Bibb & Fairly Odd Film Productions, Chantal Noordeloos, Dana Wright, Sarah.E.Glenn, Emily Hill, Luca Rossi, Matt Shoard & Fleeting Books (literary consultancy), Horror-Writers.net, Dana Schaff and the team at Fiction Terrifica, Armada West, Dr. John Dee, Edward Kelley, Dark Moon books, Andy at UK Horror-scene, Joe at Sub-Verse Magazine, Jeani Rector, Charles Bennett, Johann Schmueser, Adam 'Snuffy' Smith, Glyn Davies, Jada Ryker, Louise Simpson, Lori Michelle, Black Cat Horror, Thomas O' Brien, Simon Marshall-Jones, Alex. S. Johnson, Stuart Keane, Amanda M Lyons, J. Ellington Ashton Press, Laura Kitchell, Lisa Dabrowski and Rated Z publications, Carol Evans, Melissa, Ian Peniket, Jenna Mae, Freya, Darkworks Entertainments LLC, Dark Realms magazine, and many thanks & much appreciation to my followers & fans the readers who support the wonderful world that is Horror. If I have missed anybody, you know who you are...

A.C (JANUARY, 2015)

CHAPTER 1

As wind swept through the midst of the midnight hour, with only a sound of rattling trash cans and cats that prowl Denver street nearly every night, an echo of footsteps began from the corner of the street, as if someone was about to run to catch the last train home. Out of the shadow, from a distance, a figure in black panted like a tired dog with his leather gloved hand shifting through a dark trouser leg pocket, as if seeking some money. A blood-stained blade appeared, however, while a hellish scream kissed the night in a tormented moment of glory. The slim-looking shadow of a man began to laugh while shining his blood-stained weapon.

'What just happened? I cannot believe I just had another nightmare! It's always the same. Damn! I've got to get ready for another day at the studio.' Said Simon Kessler.

Simon had an athletic physique and stood about six feet tall. He wore his blonde hair short and enjoyed a very good complexion. He took pride in his appearance at all times, but he was also a man on a very important mission, especially during his Television broadcasts as a Psychic communicating with deceased relatives of his audience. Two hours away from the five hundredth broadcasted live to a majority of cities, Simon Kessler had his work cut out for a special show with the afterlife. He wanted to express to his audience how well he could do his job. As Simon woke, disturbed by another dream, his face appeared pale as the moon, as if he had slept rough on the sinister streets.

'Is that the time? I only have an hour to get ready and to show the population how good I can do this!'

He dragged himself out of bed and he went to the bathroom to freshen up for the forthcoming event. Simon donned his favourite pinstripe suit and his shiny, carvela shoes. He looked like a member of the Sicilian mafia.

'These shoes look very familiar,' he said as he began searching within his suit pocket for his business diary. Eventually he got himself together to go to work and headed directly into his kitchen for a quick fix of Oreo biscuits and tropical juice. He was starting to panic because he did not want to miss the event deadline. He was quickly drinking the fruit juice when the glass slid out of his grip and shattered on the floor with a deafening impact.

'Shit! I'll clean that up later,' he said while he shuffled in his pocket for his wagon keys.

A bit nervous of what might become of him after the show, he popped the lid from a bottle of anti-depressants given to him by his Manager/Agent, Mr.Jack Hodges. In his car, and about to rev up his engine, he startled when his phone began to ring. It was his Manager.

He instantly answered his phone,

'Simon, where are you? This is your special moment, so please get your ass over here to make history!' said Mr.Jack Hodges whom was always impatient and thought he was above most in his profession of reality television media.

'I would be halfway there if you didn't keep pestering me. See you shortly, Jack.' Said Simon in a hurried voice, while he began his short journey to the Television Studios.

On his way, he felt a little drowsy due to the anti-depressant tablets he had taken, and they also gave him a frequent food craving. He decided to stop by at Duquette's French café for a quick sandwich of his favourite, a cheese and red onion chutney on wholemeal bread. He slapped his face to keep awake.

'Stay awake. Not long to go now, and it will soon be over.' He said, giving himself some relief. Within a matter of minutes, he reached the studios. He carried a good luck charm which he kept close to his chest pocket daily and kissed it every morning without fail. The charm was given to him by his spiritual guru and friend.

Finally, Simon arrived and wanted to park his wagon near the entrance of the studio complex. The building was of an enormous structure, dome-shaped with a huge metal framework that resembled a dungeon. Atop the building was a sign large enough to be seen for miles. It read '**Spectrum Network Communications Centre**'. The fact that the car park was in total gridlock and the centre's futuristic and alien-like appearance made Simon more nervous than ever. Huge revolving doors allowed him to see a modernised shopping centre, and an ornamental water fountain with a statue of Nostradamus whom was an ancient Prophet from a region of France. By the revolving doors, Jack Hodges walked back and forth at a brisk pace, making a call on his cell phone. Simon waved at Jack, trying very hard to grab his attention. When this didn't work, Simon, whose mission was to satisfy his audience and make a very good impression, started to shout at Jack.

'Hey! I'm here!'

When Jack finally took notice, he turned his phone off.

'At last, you are here. You haven't been taking pills again? We haven't got long before the show begins. Oh, by the way, a woman rang the office asking for you'

Simon wondered who wanted to make contact at short notice.

'Did she leave any details or say what she wanted?'

'I told her to ring back when you're not too busy and told her you're a very important person,' said Jack in a jealous tone. While meditating before the show, Simon began to hear voices in his head of a strong, surreal nature. The atmosphere surrounding him grew very cold and isolated, like he wasn't alone anymore in the dressing room. Someone or something was sharing his private space with him. The room temperature was dropping at an alarming rate, and he felt more isolated than he ever had before. Being a Psychic had its advantages, but sharing his own emotions and privacy was a totally different matter, especially for him. Was it a sign from someone who had been close to him and who was trying to escape the wrong kind of spiritual path? But who? Simon continued to meditate, or at least tried to. A clear vision appeared of a silhouette- a female with long silk-like wings who stood motionless yet drawn into a pool of blood, like an Angel sinking into a swamp of evil, unnatural thoughts. Simon considered that the vision could be two spirits from the afterlife, one good and one evil, attempting to communicate with him. To send him a message of some great importance. But the time had arrived for his special show. How could he fully concentrate after such an episode? His heart pounded at a catastrophic rate while he clicked the well-manicured nails of his fidgeting hands. The time had come from Simon Kessler to enter the arena. He was like a Roman Gladiator entering a stadium with a pack of lions, but there wasn't a lion in sigh- just well-respected people who paid good money to see their favourite Television Psychic on this special anniversary. A cameraman counted down the seconds to broadcast time, 'Three, two, one, and action-!'

Simon began introducing the show.

'Hi there, and welcome to a special episode of 'The Afterlife with Simon Kessler-'

He perused the audience while his manager wore a pessimistic frown, as usual, behind the arena curtain like a scared child being punished.

CHAPTER TWO

Simon carried on talking to his audience about what a pleasure it was to have a well-deserved crowd of Spiritualists and general spectators, and began recalling how he became a Psychic in the first instance from his childhood. Soon Simon had focused his blood-red eyes on a lady sitting right on the middle row of the seating area. She was very tiny in height and had a squeaky voice to match her frail resemblance of a dwarf. She wore glasses thick-coated with dust.

'I have made contact with a person whose name is Sharky. I believe Sharky is connected to that lady sitting over there,' said Simon to the frail female.

'Who left a message for me?' asked the old lady, baffled to be the first chosen from the large crowd. Simon's head swelled with thoughts from the unknown, like an invisible entity was climbing and massaging his mind with nightmarish cramps.

'What is your name, sweetheart?' Simon asked the little old woman.

'My name is Gracie Richards' replied the lady, starting to get upset. She became very emotional, reminiscing about her loved one and how things could have been avoided.

'I know who he is! It's my son who tragically got killed about a month ago. His name was Marc Richards.'

An explosive connection within the arena sent Simon flashing images of a disastrous kind. His whole body began to shudder as if he were having an epileptic fit. He remembered something about that name, Marc Richards, but he could not fit the piece together.

He was still in shock from the vision he'd had in the dressing room. He craved a break from reality and wanted to run out of the building. He had a job to do, however, and he did his job well. He quickly finished the conversation with Gracie, and began to hear another voice very similar to a recent vision. This time, the message got stronger and more powerfully affective-so disturbing he thought he had entered another dimension or realm. With the show almost halfway through, Simon just wanted to get the hell out of there. He shook with frustration and nervousness. The visions returned, but, this time, a voice accompanied them. Not any voice, but a soothing, angelic tone. He began to feel at ease as the show came to an end. In an act of desperation, he sought his cold-looking, confined dressing room in the hopes of refreshing himself. A sound cable nearly tripped him, which he didn't like one bit because he would ruined his shiny, gangster-looking Carvela shoes. As he readied to leave and head to his empty lost home, the angelic voice surrounded him. That he had a very good idea who called out to him from the other side, left him in a state of shock.

'Isabelle. Isabelle,' echoed the spirit directly to Simon's mind.

He recognized the name. He really knew who it was, but he could not believe his own luck or imagination. The spirit belonged to the woman whom he'd loved for such a long time. He only had to try and remember everything and piece it altogether. He could feel himself falling into another nervous breakdown, but he had to pull himself together because he wanted to learn more about these spiritual visions, the good thoughts with the disturbingly dark. He picked up his wagon keys and the long coat he left at the reception area on his way in-the same coat he had bought for his first Psychic broadcasting.

CHAPTER THREE

As Simon drove home, his phone rang. It was Jack, and this time, he was overcome with worry about the events which had just happened. When Simon answered his phone, his body and mind suddenly felt lost forever. He sensed he was about to have an emotional breakdown. It brought with it an overwhelming sense of negativity, like he sank in a secluded pool of bitter isolation with tormented terror.

'You have not got a damn clue, have you?' asked Jack.

'What about?' replied Simon.

'The lady you spoke to in the crowd. It was her beloved son who murdered your wife-to be!' shouted Jack in an abrupt tone.

Confusion clouded Simon's mind. He had been living in denial in a long, lost journey of suffering and memory loss. Reeling from the shock, Simon felt weak and feverish while driving along on the hazardous expressway. He had to stop the wagon and collect his thoughts, including those precious moments. Sitting alongside the roadway, he stared unseeing. In a quick flash, he began to experience those tormented, reconstructed events that led to Isabelle's demise. Sharp flashes of light, like lightning had struck the eye of his mind, sent Simon into a nauseating frenzy of isolated, damned fury, as if he were trying to climb from a downward spiral. Somehow, he managed to pull into the expressway traffic and make his way to his exit. Within thirty breathless minutes, he pulled in front of Burt's general store. This was the place where Simon used to buy his fire juice, as Isabella used to call it because it was a concoction that burnt their mouths. Simon went into the store to ask for fire juice, but the place was empty. Fridges of stocked food smelled like road kill or decomposed rotted flesh, and even death. He noticed a bread rack on the right, behind the cashier counter, was infested with shivering bugs laying eggs into nesting dough within loaves of crusty bread. Simon began to have another vision, or an illusion. The exact strange black shadow of a figure, which looked very similar to the person within his recent dark dreams, appeared to him.

'Hello, what do you want? Get away from me!' howled Simon in a raging furious fit of panic. He scrambled out of the store and instantly felt light-headed as if the world closed in on him with a bursting sensation of relief. Passers-by in the street cast him peculiar looks, as if he had grown two heads and become a sideshow circus freak. Feeling weak and feverishly hot, Simon fell to the concrete with a tremendous bang like a free-falling spiritual sky diver striking the ground of disillusioned reality. He woke hours later with concussion from the blow to his head. He no longer lay on the pavement outside Burt's general store but was in a very strange place, a place didn't recognize. He called out, but no reply answered, so he studied the surreal surroundings. He became frozen within his stare with a thought of trembling fear. Simon found himself within a clinical bed and could clearly see a straitjacket hanging from a creaking cupboard door.

Obviously, he knew this was used to restrain patients, or a convict of mental health. He soon realized this was a mental asylum. An unusual scent of paint thinner brought to mind a pharmacy counter with strong ingredients which were tested on humans for a scientific and chemical reaction. He tried to circulate movement in his arms but felt very numb. He was strapped down on the bed within this psychiatric Hospital. He shouted, demanding answers. Suddenly he awoke from an unconscious state. How long had he slept? His room contained various equipment which were used when interrogating some vicious criminal. Did they doctors want to find information from his Psychic mind? Simon just wanted to learn how he'd gotten to this strange place. Still semi-drowsy, he let his gaze travel the walls of the Hospital room.

A hall of fame style notice board hung next to the door on the left hand side near the suffocating bed where he lay. His heart pounded as if he was about to have a lapse, probably due to the amount of medication he took before his show. He read the notice board.

'Meadow Hall Medical Centre- Psychiatric/Analysis Centre'

Simon went limp, overcome by a dreary state of mind. Clinging to consciousness, he noticed a green switch located at the side of this bed. He pressed the switch six times, and a tall, slender nurse came to his room. She wore a uniform similar to a female Naval Officer, and she strutted into the room like an Executive Secretary with a very important role. The nurse glanced at Simon, while checking out the patient assessment located at the bottom of his bed and making notes. Simon suffered a surge of anxiety. Why was he in this place?

'Hello, can you tell me how I got here please?' yelled Simon.

'Oh! Sorry. You had a fall and behaved rather strange outside the store,' replied the nurse.

'You were acting and behaving very strangely and talking to yourself, saying that a black shadow was following you.'

'Can you tell me when I can go from here please?' screamed Simon. The atmosphere around him grew quite weary, but he only wanted to find what happened to his lady the day before their wedding. He continued to ask questions to the Nurse about how he could get the hell out of there and to concentrate on his next project, which was scheduled to air live around the world, a project which no other Psychic had ever tried and succeeded to do previously.

'Hello will I be able to leave here today please?' asked Simon.

The nurse reached in her pocket and withdrew a blood-soaked blade, which she dragged against the fabric of her garment.

'It's ok. It's your time to die now, Simon.' She said.

Within a split second, the nurse's actions became transfixed from the hypnotising crimson coloured knife, as if a blood drenched cloud appeared around her, she now had a resemblance like a twisted, psychopathic killer with piercing demonic eyes along with her voice changing while she laughed devilishly. It became deeper and haunting by the second. And her eyes turned bloodshot with an image of a deeply penetrated bullet wound.

Simon had to get out of there fast. He used a form of mind control, which he learnt from a friend and soul mate, Augustus, to distract the nurse. He focused and emptied every thought, concentrating very intensively. Even though telepathy of the mind was a very tiring practice, he was determined to escape. Simon began controlling an operation of mind communications. It dawned on him that an evil spirit now possessed the Nurse to get to him.

'Who is this wanting my presence? Why? I will not kneel for you! Please leave this body at once!' Simon called through his telepathic link.

He lifted his tired leg and kicked the Nurse, repelling this spiritual formation into chaos. The Nurse became delirious, letting go of the blade which landed next to Simon's hand. Simon grabbed the knife and cut the leather strapping from his wrists and freed himself from the bed. He ran to the doorway, but there were people everywhere. Simon located his clothing and quickly dressed and then went to an emergency window near to the miserable bed. Making an escape through the small framed window, he discovered a rotating stairwell which lead to the ground floor located next to the car park. He noticed his wagon parked up which was a strange coincidence. Simon ran to the security of his own vehicle. The keys were dangled in the car door, which made his life much easier, considering the state he was in. He realised he was followed by the Nurse because her photo id appeared on the dashboard. He climbed into the vehicle and started the ignition and heard a spiritual voice communicating with him. He looked out the window, but nobody was about. Had he lost his mind, or was he just heavily sedated by the Nurse he had encountered?

'Simon. Get out of here. Go now.' Said the whispering voice.

He knew he had to get of there, this spiritual being must have been in his presence the whole time.

'Hello. I have heard your voice before and it seems extremely familiar,' replied Simon to this entity.

'I am Isabelle,' said the spirit.

Simon did not know what the hell he was doing, or what the hell he was going to do, but he had to get the fuck away from there. Though he was still slightly drowsy, he managed to rev the wagon's engine and drive toward home, his hands shook nervously and his heart was racing fast. He was trying to figure out the voice of Isabelle, and why now he suddenly heard her. Trying to catch his breath, finally he arrived at the house feeling shocked and incredibly hungry. He fixed a quick bite to eat and contemplated what to do next. Then he recalled Jack telling him a woman had left a very important message for him. he immediately headed towards his phone to check his voicemails. To his amazement, he had a hundred messages, mainly from clients from his weekend psychic hotline. Simon sat in his leather armchair and played every single message. On several occasions, the same person had left thirty calls. He reached into his long coat and find the special fountain pen gifted him from a client.

The pen must have been damaged when he escaped from the psychiatric hospital because ink leaked through his coat and soaked his shirt through. He reached deeper into his coat and felt something cold and sharp. Simon pulled the object from his pocket. It was the knife from the nightmarish episodes, by now he was too tired to panic. A closer look revealed three letters inscribed on the handle of the blade. Simon dashed to the kitchen to wash the stale-smelling blood from the knife and to see more clearly if he could find some clue to solve the puzzle of the three letters. He scrubbed very hard, using an acidic cleaner. His hands became irritated with burning sensations and blisters because of the powerful corrosive substance. Soon, the letters began to appear visible.

'S.R.S,' said Simon. Were they a person's initials? Could it even be a clue toward resolving Isabelle's murder?

CHAPTER FOUR

The recent events now intensely pressurized Simon's thoughts. He went to his study room adjacent to the kitchen, but the room was very small and cluttered from floor to ceiling with books, study notes and manuscripts which dated back more than one hundred and fifty years of research into sciences and psychic abilities and spiritual meditation. Simon turned the switch on to his computer, extremely anxious and full of curiosity to find out more about the letters 'S.R.S,'.

He typed the letters into the internet search engine and clicked the search button. While the engine searched for the letters, Simon headed back to his voicemails and replayed them. He hoped for some answers. Jennie Simmonds had left several messages. She was a long-time friend of both Isabelle's and his. They attended the same college together and been friends from that moment. Her messages held an air of urgency and desperation.

'Simon. It's been a long time since we last met up together, and I think you should come over here as I have some very important to tell you. So get over to my house as quickly as you can,' said Jennie in a dominating manner.

Just before he went to get organized to go to Jennie's, he returned to his computer. Only two search results appeared on the screen. He became overwhelmed to find out the letters were an abbreviation for some-kind of a secret society or brotherhood of immortality with destructive ideas.

Frustration mixed with anger, joy and total confusion. He wondered if Jennie might know of this secret order and what they wanted with him. His main question, however, why was he, of all people ended up with this blade? Jennie could help him because she had studied history at Hillfort University. If anyone knew resources about this kind of subject, Jennie did. She definitely hid something of a dark and sinister nature, if her tone in the messages she'd left were any indication. When Simon was about to leave for Jennie's house, the phone rang. It was his manager Jack. He might has well answer it to get everyone off his back so his manager would not become suspicious.

'Hey, Jack, I want some time off. Let's say a week, because I need to collect my thoughts and to balance my psychic energies. You don't mind, do you?' Simon asked.

'Go ahead. You read my mind. No pun intended. You need a break, and good luck' replied Jack.

Simon changed into a black suit, actually a wedding suit, and he wanted to feel comfortable and full of karma. He looked so immaculate and clean, like the Don from the Godfather movie. He picked up is wagon keys, went to his car, and started the engine. He had no idea what was going to happen, but he had a sense he was living in a nightmare, or a beginning of a secret conspiracy. He began to feel rather feverish and started to tremble, like the very nervous child he'd been while attending Wychbury School. Bullying had occurred most days due to the other boy's fascination with his ability to communicated with the dead. He realized he was quite a lost soul of a man, even in recent years while studying in advanced psychic awareness studies.

 Simon instantly revved the engine, having forgotten to take the handbrake off. He journeyed the hours toward Jennie's house. The weather was changing quickly and drastically. A cold mist was beginning to appear in the far distance over the picturesque landscape. The only sounds he heard were the howls of an evening wolf pack, and his psychic mind knew they called out in hunger for a blooded corpse of a defenceless and innocent animal which was killed by a local deer hunter for pleasure. If he could have communicated with dead animals, he suspected they would have a lot of educative words to say. Thirty minutes into the journey, Simon pulled the wagon over to the side of the road near a truck stop. The erratic wolf cries screamed through the walls of his ears. It was still becoming colder. The temperature on the monitor of his wagon fluctuated between -5, and -8 degrees. Still he could not stop that erratic sound. He managed to find some thermal gloves and put them on and then rubbed his ears red raw. He called Jennie on his phone and told her he was delayed for a while. His voice was slowly crackling and breaking away, making it difficult to talk right.

'Jennie, I...it's Simon, I....will be delayed. See you soon.' Simon was freezing.

The temperature monitor fluctuated at a faster pace, so he clenched his cold fist and banged the screen of the monitor with anger. Then the temperature began to increase, and the mist faded into the distance as if time was reversing. The howling began again, and he knew the current moment in this present time was at a standstill. Simon Kessler continued his most bizarre journey to Jennie's house. He had never felt a spiritual cosmic force like this, not even during his psychic television broadcastings. It occurred to him he'd forgotten his tablets, which is so-called perfect manager, Jack, gave to him to deal with his problems.

He was of two minds-whether to head back home and fetch his medicine or to carry on and drive to Jennie's. he had grown so dependent on them. After all, they helped him through the breakdown due to Isabelle's killing. Even her death was covered up. As every hour passed, Simon's memory gradually returned. He didn't need the tablets. He was becoming more in control of his life and gaining self-confidence. Even though he was beginning to remember certain memories from his history, he still had a notion of a blackout happening, hanging over him like a formidable shadow from his past. He parked his vehicle on the grit road and began to walk the remaining journey to Jennie's house, which was only a short breathless distance away. As he strode at a quick pace, his chest was suffocating in a strenuous motion and that left him panting and shaking with fear in a schizophrenic episode endured within madness.

Finally, he reached the end of those miles of desperation, as if he reached the finish line in a dehydrating marathon. In difficult circumstances, he liked to carry with him his Grandfather's bible, but present distractions, he didn't think to collect it from the house.

As Simon reached the bottom of the foggy hill, his throat became dry as a human bone. He wiped his mouth, and his skin cracked from the dryness of his lips. His feet flamed like a scorching sun roasting on the desert plains. He began to walk like a zombie with stiffness and cramp-pulled muscles in his whole shivering body. Jennie's house came into view, situated at an old rail crossings which hadn't seen use in over two hundred years. Jennie lived in a peaceful town with a dense population of Preachers. An old tale from locals insisted the place had once been a magic playground for pagan witches. However, Simon wasn't too bothered. He just wanted to collapse from severe exhaustion. As he reached the front doorway of Jennie's home, Simon noticed traditional wind chimes, which native Indian tribes once used to contact their deceased ancestors for guidance and support. His friend had always been fascinated with different cultural beliefs and magic traditions, after being abandoned by her family when she was a baby. It had changed her perception on life forever.

All she wanted was fulfilment and a clear spiritual path for her journey in life and beyond. She must have worked hard over the years, because Jennie had a large house with a sauna and steam room. The structure was nostalgic in colonial standards of designs. It had once been owned by the Beaumont Family who traded in sugar and grain production, while using a number of African slaves for a cheap labour. It had worked very well, indeed. Simon knocked upon the large lead-framed door, and the sound echoed like thunder. It met with no reply, so he went to the side of the house and tried to visualise where she was. He heard Peruvian pan-pipes and banged harder on the iced-glassed surfaced window.

'Hello! Who's there?' shouted Jennie.

'Let me in. It's Simon!'

He hurried back to the front doorway.

'Oh, bloody shit! Haven't seen you in a damn long time! Come inside. You look like hell'

Jennie's expression looked like she was high, because she slightly mumbled when she spoke, and she was dressed like a hippie flower girl, wearing hot pants. Simon stepped inside and immediately collapsed on the floor. As Simon woke from his exhaustive collapse, he noticed she had tucked him in a large bed with thermal blankets which were becoming rather heavy and hot.

The crackling sound of the log fire came from a fireplace in the corner of the resting room. The fragrance of incense surrounded him, vaporising like a rising mist around the room. It was probably to ward off evil entities of a spiritual nature. Simon strained to get out of the bed to find Jennie. He followed the sound of panpipes. Jennie kneeled on the floor while exercising ancient yogic techniques. It was quite relaxing for him to observe this, especially considering how the mind could be changed through various lessons of thought and control. This was exactly what Simon needed in order to grasp onto reality and to make him feel complete and stronger, as a psychic and a man.

'Wow! This is so calming, Jennie,' he said, interrupting the last part of her routine. Jennie pulled herself up from her yoga practice. She seemed refreshed and full of life, please to see him on his feet, she shows Simon her dragon tattoo on her inner thigh, which she had during the old school days.

'Are you any feeling better, Simon? You look like you're hungry,' Jennie said, showing him hospitality and care for his wellbeing. He slowly followed her into the Greek structured marble kitchen.

CHAPTER FIVE

While in the kitchen, Jennie walked over to a huge American-style fridge full of food, enough to cater for a restaurant filled with people. She had prime steaks and various vegetarian foods.

'I have your favourite rib eye steak here,' said Jennie.

'I'm thrilled to have a guest, especially an old chum like you. We can chat all day and night about memories.'

She had always been a talkative girl, even in her college days, always the girl at the centre of attention for every college football boy. When they sat down to eat dinner, Jennie began to tell Simon a few truths and her theory behind Isabelle's murder. Jennie has always been honest and quick to the point when it came to most subjects. She asked him about his fame as a television psychic and what he liked about doing that profession in front of a huge audience and if he ever had a nervous disposition about communicating with the afterlife. Treating her like someone who had a school crush on him, Simon was very expressive and approachable. The mood of the discussion gradually changed when Jennie began to talk about Isabelle and her thoughts on how she sadly died, which was still mysterious for Simon. He went to the bathroom to freshen up and gazed into the cold-looking mirror, hoping to find life's answer or some comfort to make him feel at ease while talking to Jennie. The conversation was about to get deeper, and Simon had to be ready for what he was about to hear. He suspected something would come as a shock. Back at the dinner table, Jennie started to tell Simon some baffling truths about his manager, Jack Hodges. She mentioned how she tried to contact Simon over a month ago, and how Jack used to verbally abuse Isabelle over a certain secret that he wanted and which was a matter of life and death. Being Jennie, she just came out with all this information, whether it hurt his feelings or not. She was a very honest person when it concerned the welfare of Isabelle and Simon, and she had planned to be Isabelle's bridesmaid at their wedding. She wanted Simon to know about the arguments and harassment that Isabelle had suffered from his devious manager.

'I have to tell you something Isabelle told me before she died,' said Jennie.

While Simon listened, Jennie scraped her nervous long nails on the dining table. Her decorative nails mesmerised him. The scraping reminded him of how Isabelle used to have the same habit, especially when she had an important question to ask.

'Simon, are you listening to me?' asked Jennie urgently and persistently then waited for his response.

'I am listening, just mesmerised of how you have the same habit of scraping your nails on the table, the same as Isabelle did,' replied Simon as he reminisced about the love he had for Isabelle. He became emotionally frustrated and trembled with tears, while scratching his right leg. Isabelle was his lifetime companion and realising that part of him was no longer there, he was in need of Samaritan advice from Jennie. Simon couldn't cope on his own, and not having his tablets made him feel more lonely, more abstract from life. Though his thoughts had become clearer and stronger since he stopped taking the last tablets. He asked Jennie for a glass of iced water with a hint of lemon, the way Isabelle used to make it. Isabelle used to crush the ice, which was more soothing for Simon's throat dryness, and affliction he'd suffered since childhood. Jennie gave Simon his iced water, which he desperately drank to calm his nerves.

'Are you ready to hear what I have got to say?' Jennie asked.

'Will you just tell me, Jennie? I have been going out of mind about what's been happening,' replied Simon, gasping for air. Jennie began to tell him about Jack and how he wasn't the person Simon thought he was. Simon listened raptly.

'About a month ago, Isabelle came to my house in a state of

panic. It was raining very hard outside. The rain bounced off the ground, and I heard constant banging on the front of the veranda. I was in a state of undress at the time, as you remember when we used to have nights of naked games. Anyway, I went to the door, and Isabelle was drenched through like a drowned rat. I asked her what happened, and she told me that your manager, Jack, is an evil and corrupt man. Jack wanted to make a deal with Isabelle so you could have a major broadcasting career,' said Jennie to a Simon's shock. Jennie carried on with her information. Simon had a perfect right to know what might have contributed to his lover's sadistic death. But he had some questions.

'I do not understand all of this. So you're basically telling me that my psychic career has been a joke all of this time?' Simon couldn't curb his angry tone. He was just beginning to get his head around what Jennie told him, and he was only now realising certain normalities like those tablets given to him by Jack Hodges. Why had Jack given him those tablets? Simon had thought they were genuine medicine, but obviously they weren't. Now Simon examined his real thoughts and actions, and reconstructed past events over the last weeks.

'When I think about those tablets Jack gave me, I realise he told me they were for my nerves. But when I accidentally forgot my tablets on my way down here to your house, I started to see everyday things and situations in a whole new and clear light. Those tablets weren't for my nerves. They were erasing my thoughts and, at times, I felt so wasted, and vulnerable to most things,' said Simon.

'I know. Shall we browse the internet to find out more about this Jack Hodges?,' asked Jennie.

Then Simon remembered about the letters on the handle of that blood-drenched blade.

'Hey. I forgot to mention I ended up in hospital a few days back, and I was in such a delirious frame of mind, but I remember this nurse in particular, and she gazed at me with such a hellish presence about her. Anyway, I escaped from that shit hole then managed to drive back home and found this odd-looking knife covered in blood in my coat pocket. I discovered three letters on the handle of the blade. 'S.R.S,' said Simon in a hurried tone. She led him to her computer to try and find some answers about the recent happenings. Immediately, without hesitation, Jennie turned on her computer, and they worked together by typing various keywords to search the mysterious lettering from the bloody knife. They investigated Jack Hodges to find out who he really was, and why Isabelle suffered the way she did by Jack's cold-blooded deviousness and deception while he claimed to be true friend and business colleague to Simon. While Jennie was searching for information on the internet, Simon got to grips with himself and plucked the courage to phone his manager so he could tell him that he needed more time off from his gruelling work schedule. Simon asked Jennie if he could use her private phone line. At least that way nobody could trace his call.

'Hey! Jack, I will need more time off. I was thinking of going on a short break to Heath Cliff Bay. I will call you when I feel one hundred percent and ready to work again,' said Simon to the answer machine in Jack's office.

It was bizarre that Jack was not available to pick up his phone. He was usually on that damn thing most afternoons. In the meantime, Jennie managed to find a couple of leads about Jack. Jennie swivelled her chair and said in a sarcastic tone,

'You will never guess what I have just found about beloved.'

'What have you found? Tell me!' Simon replied impatiently.

'I have found where Jack is currently living, and he certainly has a secret to hide. No wonder he tried to cover up the truth of his family tradition within a secret order,' said Jennie.

'We need to learn about this secret and if there are connections with those mysterious letters, S.R.S'

Their stress levels were making them slightly nauseated and frustrated. Simon found information of a startling nature, more sinister and disastrous than a normal Psychic's mind could handle. He became feverish and hot blooded explaining to Jennie, in a wallowing state of mind,

'I can't believe this!' he said.

'Listen to this. There is an ancient religious order based near the broadcasting studios, and basically they control the government police and fire services. It also says this 'Sanctuary of the Red Sun' has been around since the beginning of Christianity and they began their so-called religious systems on the dawn of western religion and civilisation.' Jennie showed signs of anguish and tiredness, as if she had foreseen these events from her deep philosophical life of study. Simon read more and noted that the 'Sanctuary of the Red Sun' had established themselves from jealousy and they felt immortalised at the sudden death of Christ. By the end of the holy wars, they wanted to control every subject in their path, whether to control human minds or greed of financial markets. Soon after, they began to operate in underground networks. Most members of the S.R.S. were wealthy and powerful individuals who wanted to control the world and to invent a scientific device that controlled thoughts, emotions and to steal classified ideas of religious importance. Simon browsed more resources relating to this webpage until he began to realise his whole Psychic career was a media joke. His manager and Psychic team were just devious meddling abusers.

CHAPTER SIX

Simon felt mental stress and torment, not just from the facts he had discovered and from the strain of being psychically and mentally used, but also from the shocking implications behind the death of Isabelle. She had been his ultimate gift of love, and a lifetime companion. Jennie insisted it would be a great idea to travel to Heath Cliff Bay, situated near a former Indian reservation located in Connecticut, and stay a few days. It seemed an idealistic place to venture due to the hollowed and spiritual ground blessed by the tribespeople. Within a few hours of trying to clarify his thoughts, Simon quickly became motivated like a kid in a candy store. Jennie began to pack and gather emergency phone numbers, just in case something bad happened along the way to the hallowed ground of Heath Cliff Bay. Simon and Jennie embarked on their journey of blissful escapism.

They had to travel through the cursed town of Salem, a town noted for the burning of witches and for uses of instruments of horrifying torture and the arson of family homes. They decided to catch a few hours of sleep before their journey ahead. During the midnight hour, not a sound could be heard other than the rustling noise of local vermin and neighbourhood cats tearing through trashcans in search of their pot of gold or luck in finding a bloodthirsty feast. Simon left his bedroom open while, elsewhere in the suburbs, wind pressure began to increase at a fast pace of heavens fury. Simon settled under the thermal bed covers and slowly drifted into a dream state. Within a few moments, his whole body began to travel into an astral path of spiritual unknowing and self-exploration, into his deepest memories and realistic thoughts. Even creatures of the night outside the frosted window scattered because they felt a powerful presence of evil or demonic occurrence. The following morning, Jennie woke much earlier than dreary eyed Simon. It only took her ten minutes to pack their three large luggage cases and two toiletry bags, mostly filled with Jennie's health and wellbeing pills. Simon always travelled light with only his laptop, pens and notebook, wearing just the clothes he'd arrived in. He had an early morning craving of ham and cheese, which reminded him of his forever love for his departed Isabelle. The weather changed, bringing the sounds of crackling grey skies with a vibrating sound like crunching feet on seashells. They were ready for the journey to Heath Cliff Bay but, with this disturbing weather approaching, it distracted Simon's abilities to concentrate on spiritual and metaphysical subjects.

He had always suffered terrible migraines, too. Since childhood, he constantly worried over the slightest problem. Jennie insisted they go, however. On their journey to the bay, the radio frequency kept switching to disastrous events which had taken place over the years. Simon clenched his hand and banged the radio on the dashboard of the vehicle. He became incredibly hot and feverish, panting like a dog for its water bowl. Jennie noticed the road sign to Heath Cliff Bay, which stated they were now only a few miles from their destination. The radio frequency returned to normal, as if nothing happened, like an hallucination had vanished through a bad nightmare. Simon and Jennie agreed they felt they were on a journey to hell. Heath Cliff Bay was located in a flamboyant for tourists because of its atmosphere and surroundings of bizarre witchcraft practices involving sacrificial ceremonies of religious preachers. As Simon and Jennie arrived, the weather opened like an envelope of sunshine and clear blue crystal skies.

'Smell that beautiful fresh sea air, Jennie' said Simon with a relaxed tone.

They gathered their luggage from the vehicle and headed to the entrance of the reception of the Portland Hotel, located near Heath Cliff Woods where they would stay for the next couple of days to resolve their anguish and get to grips with certain scenarios which lay ahead. That night, while the majority of the world slept like clockwork robots to fund the government, Simon had visionary thoughts of the past. Suddenly he sensed the presence of his grandfather. He had been very close to his grandfather as a child, or what he could remember, anyway. Simon was transported through to events when he was a child, and he noticed many people standing in a Victorian study room which resembles a lavish house from a televised costume drama with pristine decorations and blooming floral arrangements. A very strong smell of wood polish filled the space, and the sound was to a minimum. Not even the sound of the rustling wind outside could be heard. Elsewhere in the study room, a huge table positioned in the centre of the room was placed directly under a ceiling with symbolic letterings engraved onto a series of oak beamed objects which formed a pattern of a tree. The tree looked like a historical timeline or a pathway for magical knowledge and achievement.

Simon also noticed within this eerie study room that many people stood around this table of great importance, as if in a celebration of life and birth. But in fact, there was about to be a spiritual awakening and an initiation of a rebirth of esoteric knowledge of high proportions. Various Egyptian artefacts and ceremonial instruments used for the gainful attention of the holy guardian angel and practices for attainment of Enochian magick were present. Simon Kessler woke from his transfixed distorted visions and recalled what he had just witnessed and foreseen.

He didn't want to wake Jennie since they'd had such a long journey to the Portland Hotel. He quickly got his pen and notebook from the side table in his hotel room and made a strong coffee as he began to make notes and try to work out the visions from moments ago. He remembered an item his grandfather had given to him many years back, which he stored hidden behind a picture frame of Isabelle and himself taken on a romantic holiday.

He had to get back to his home to get this special item, but first, he had to wake Jennie from her sleep next door. After Simon dressed and packed his pens and notepads, he went to knock upon Jennie's door. Her door was already open, however, and Jennie was in a nervous panic. Sweat flowed from her brow, as if she suffered from a sudden heatwave. But he had no time to waste in dealing with Jennie's emotions and problems at the moment. He had

captured in in an expression of true natural beauty. As Simon reached under the brass picture frame, he felt an utter, bitter coldness within himself, though he finally found what he sought. An Enochian magick scroll was secured in an old snakeskin leather trunk his grandfather had stored many years ago with other various secret items such as talismans and ancient relics. These items could be made more powerful by magicians who trained and studied hard on a daily basis with the initiated attainment given like a scholar ranking into a higher grade. Simon grabbed the storage trunk and sat on the bed while opening the lock. While opening the lid, he cut his hand on the sharp metallic edge which lined the case. The palm of his left hand spurted out streams of blood.

Simon drifted into a sudden dream of peaceful surrender, quivering right down to his aching and tired feet. Within his dream state vision, he wasn't alone. Something else awaited his presence. Something which he clearly didn't recognise from his own psychic awareness. This was more powerful, and he knew at this moment he was about to find out more about the mysteries surrounding many hidden happenings and certain evils directed not just at him but at his whole family, too.

'Oh, no. What is happening?' asked Simon nervously. He began to tremble profusely. Simon was tormented to witness before his tired and alerted eyes that some kind of judgment day was approaching. He sat on the edge of the four-poster bed in an unconscious state of mind. A dark mist became a shape shifting image. He could also hear a faint scream from a distance. A screeching voice in tremendous pain and torment became louder. Much louder. It came closer, speaking words not from this world. Simon ran out of the house as quick as he could while clenching the trunk under his arm. Outside, he could still hear the words. Simon went straight to the wreck of the vehicle so he could make a note of these mysterious words. He tried to open the door, but it was jammed so tightly due to the damage. Another sound reached him, and it was coming from the engine. He also realised the smell of oil was getting stronger. He had to hurry. He yanked on the door as forcefully as he could, but it refused to open. He sensed that he didn't have much time, and he knew he had to be as quick as possible. Simon was sweating and becoming breathless, frustrated and angry. An urgency told him he only as seconds to open the door. The clock was ticking faster, and he was becoming disorientated. As the smell got stronger and the time grew closer, Simon had to get away from there quickly. He couldn't open the door, and he could see the pen and notebook resting on the passenger seat where Jennie had previously sat.

Simon shouted, 'Oh, for fuck's sake! Why can't anything go well in my personal life?' He began to run.

He ran like an athlete for his life and safety. A crashing and explosive bang erupted through his beloved vehicle. He couldn't look back and risk losing focus on where he was running to. Dark smoldered ash from the explosion landed on his face. Simon needed to rest a moment because he was breathless and dehydrated. He was also very tired though grateful enough to still have the important trunk in his possession. But, there was another problem. He had left his phone upstairs in the house, and he was too exhausted to make his way back. Even if he did, he was very unsure of what might happen. Firstly, he had to think of where he could make a note of the words he had just received from the spiritual being. He slowly walked along Denver Street. It was usually quiet and ambient on this street, but today, it was very loud and socially noisy, which baffled Simon. He carried on walking until he stood outside a religious house where a group of four females and one male occupied the wall surrounding the house. Owned by a church pastor and his wife. Simon became disillusioned as he drifted slowly past the house. His footsteps echoed. The atmosphere began to change. Something odd was happening in front of his eyes.

CHAPTER EIGHT

Simon stood outside the Pastor's house and gazed in utter amazement. He needed to use a phone to call Jennie and to write down the message he received a few moments ago, and he knew it was a matter of urgency. He gradually strolled up to the gang of people outside the house, completely astonished to discover that the one man in that group was the Pastor. He was arousing himself and appeared in a stargazing trance. Simon was devastated and shocked by how the Pastor was behaving. Everyone in the neighbourhood knew Pastor Maxwell. He was a short man and well reserved, devoting his entire life to his religious beliefs in Christianity. He once ran for congress within the community because the local people believed and trusted in him. He was always a man to keep communication in confidence. Simon had heard rumours that Pastor Maxwell belonged to the Illuminati, whom are a secret society within the United States of America. Simon immediately approached Pastor Maxwell to ask if everything was okay and if he could use his telephone and to make a few notes. He hadn't recognised the Pastor because the man didn't wear his usual church clothing. Instead, he wore dark leather shorts which incredibly tight like cyclist's shorts. Simon didn't know whether to laugh in amazement or be mortified upon seeing him dressed in this way.

With a giggle, he said, 'I don't have this problem when I am at my naturist beach. I am so thankful for that. Wow!'

The thought passed, as Simon had to concentrate on more important things. The evening had a slight chill in the air, which was another reason why he found Pastor Maxwell's attire shocking. He was not dressed accordingly with the right climate.

'Pastor Maxwell, how are you, Sir?' said Simon.

The atmosphere had a sudden sense of a daze and a flutter of odd confusion. The Pastor looked like he had been drinking or if he had been to a party. The man swayed and mumbled in an array of babbling words like a slobbering youth. Surrounding the well-respected Pastor was the group of four females who seemed mischievous and lively in their nearness to Pastor Maxwell. The women wore skimpy, exotic, dark latex clothing, and one of them held a very unusual looking whip as if for some form of punishment. It was also made from leather. The girls all resembled each other, like quadruplet sisters. Simon felt he was in some kind of illusion or a nightmare from a world like no other. Two of the exotic girls had their hands on the Pastor's rear. Simon smelled drugs coming from the Pastor's house, which had a French style structure with Tudor-like windows of stained glass with various religious timeline depictions. The smell became more intense, but Simon could also smell fear.

'Pastor Maxwell, what is going on here, Sir?' asked Simon in an aggravated tone.

'Hey, kid. How are ya doing?' replied the Happy Pastor.

Simon urgently shook his hand, but he was still unsure about what was happening.

'I need some help, Sir. I need help now. Right now,' Simon said, terrified.

But Pastor Maxwell appeared distracted by the exotic females which fondled him in many places.

'I just need to use your phone, Sir,' said Simon to a now very delirious Pastor Maxwell. Simon rushed past the group of females, and as he walked past them, one of the girls made a provoking comment directed at him.

'It was your fault. It was you. I can ease that pain, Simon. Want me to show you?' said the female who suddenly transformed into Isabelle.

'Isabelle, Isabelle,' replied a disillusioned Simon to the mysterious woman. He didn't know what was making him feel like this. He blinked, and Isabelle disappeared. Now it was this female who spoke to him and not his true love.

'What is happening to me? Why is this happening?' Simon asked himself.

Feeling frustrated and angry, he hurried through the front door of Pastor Maxwell's house and along the creaking wooden hallway. The hallway within the house was huge with a high beamed ceiling. European chandeliers flickered with a mesmerising light as he headed along the empty corridor of echoes. It was very quiet, and not even a whisper could be heard or an image in sight except Renaissance paintings in enormous antique frames positioned along the high walls of the corridor. As Simon walked further, he observed the paintings. The first painting featured a family portrait of a mother, father, and four identical little girls. Something looked bizarrely wrong with the painting. Firstly, it read on the frame that it had been painted during the season of winter, but the image depicted a spring or summer season with colourful blooms and birds nesting in the trees. He saw no way could this have been composed during the winter months. Also, nobody was smiling in the painting. It appeared as if something had upset them and occupied their attention. Gradually, Simon reached the end of the hallway.

The scent of drugs soon cleared. He knew where the phone was because he had visited the Pastor's house a while back to take a letter for his marriage to Isabelle. Pastor Maxwell hadn't been available at the time, so they couldn't give their vows. Instead, a Vicar from a church in the next town had accepted his letter. Finally, Simon noticed three doors on the right at the end of the hallway. They were large wooden doors with heavy brass handles, each door had some-kind of symbol engraved on them. Simon went through the third door because he knew that's where the phone was located. The living quarters of the house had a touch of elegance, with a silk lined sofa woven in an oriental fabric and an enormous oval mahogany dining table with crystal glass decanters which looked as if they hadn't been used. Each contained enough whiskey that the slightest touch would overflow the alcohol within them. Simon had a thirst for whiskey. He went to the large royal crystal decanter and softly had a sip to quench his lips and taste.

'Ah, that was just so good. Just what I needed,' he said.

He headed across the room to use the phone to contact Jennie. The phone was at the far end of the elegant–looking room. He found a pen and notepad on the small phone table, so he made notes of what happened in the past hour. He nervously grabbed the phone and quickly dialled Jennies hotel room number but there was no answer. He tried one more time. This time, a banshee answered. It was the same voice he had heard earlier that day from his house. Simon threw the phone onto the floor. Faintly, Jennie's voice called from the handset. He felt an instant moment of ease and picked the phone off the carpeted floor. Her soft-spoken voice relieved him. Simon explained to Jennie of what has been happening since he left her at the hotel earlier that day.

'I cannot believed what has happened, Jennie,' he said, upset.

While still on the phone, he poured a large whiskey into an expensive glass.

'Are you listening to me, Jennie? My car exploded, I heard a strange voice, and the local Pastor is behaving so oddly. I don't know what is happening.'

'Are you serious? I am amazed. Tell me more about this voice. I know, even better, write this down and come straight back to me. We need to look into this more,' said Jennie, her voice anxious.

'Okay. I am making a note of this right now, and I will get there as soon as I can.' Replied Simon.

He jotted down the words the best to his memory, though unsure what they meant and the meaning behind the event. Why had Isabelle been murdered? She was killed in such a brutal way. He needed resolution to the recent strange events. Simon approached the back door of the room, which had an open patio, so he could make a quick exit. Surely things couldn't get much worse. As soon as he headed outside, he noticed more people in Pastor Maxwell's back garden. The area was much a secluded garden with four flower beds of exotic and cultural floral decorations. It was colourful and blooming, full of sunshine within the well preserved garden. There were two large flower beds on each side and an extensive green lawn flowing through the centre. Also located at the end was a hot mineral tub, and he could smell floral scents and soothing minerals from the hot tub in the distance. Simon slowly walked around to the left, avoiding the people on the grass who were involved in all manners of sexualised acts with various painted images of religious symbols on their naked bodies. It brought to mind the 1960's in its complete freedom of acceptance and of drug use and certain behaviours. He pulled the notes from his pocket and continued along the left side of the wall at the back of the house. He made notes of these symbols too. They could mean something.

'Ha. Jennie would love this. Oh, my, said Simon.

He hurried to get as far from the house as possible. He didn't even say a thank you to the Pastor. But the Pastor seemed utmost distracted by those girls. When Simon was a few streets away, he was only a matter of yards from a taxi depot. He was sweating and panicking like he never had previously that day. Simon was a trembling, and tired wreck. He sensed, however, that something was about to appear out of the darkness of his mind. Something was now about to mentally change within him.

CHAPTER NINE

As Simon approached the reception counter of the taxi depot so he could book a ride to go to Jennie's hotel room, he was quivering like a nervous school boy as he dragged his worn out legs to ask the receptionist for transportation.

'Excuse me, I need a taxi please.' Said Simon to the silent lady at the desk.

He repeated his request three times until he finally got a response.

'How may I help you today?' asked the lazy receptionist.

'I need to get to the main railroad, just as you enter Massachusetts town.' He hurriedly replied.

'On its way. About five minutes,' stated the receptionist.

Simon became quite nauseated as he dragged himself backwards to the waiting area outside of the taxi depot. He could only stare at the fingers on his watch as it ticked away, as if he was a madman awaiting a countdown of extinction. The car eventually drove up to the waiting area, and Simon slowly picked himself up from the sunken leather seat. He strolled to the taxi for his journey to his friend's house. To his dismay, the driver inhaled from a cigarette.

'Do you mind, can you please put that out? He asked.

'Sure, dude.' Replied the taxi driver, hesitantly and cool.

Simon used the forty-minutes to put words together smoothly for Jennie. He glanced out the left window for a simple moment of ambience. His neck was cramping with pain now, and he felt overtired after the hectic day. Then he passed the church. He could see the group of dwellers whom were at Pastor Maxwell's house not too long ago.

'Driver, I need to get over to the church across the street. I mean now!'

'Okay, dude. Okay. What's your hurry?' asked the driver.

'Let's just say I need to get something arranged,' responded Simon as he flicked his fingers nervously through his hair.

The taxi driver took an immediate U-turn into approaching traffic, taking all manner of abuse from the annoyed drivers on the busy street. He took Simon directly to the side of the church gates, where nobody could see him coming. Simon dashed to the other side of the street and crouched down, panting like a tired dog. He rushed to the side wall of the gothic-structured church. Where a row of six tall, stained glass windows depicted Jesus Christ. He scuffled while dragging himself along the wall until he came to the last window. Underneath was a door, once used during the 1980's to assist religious travelling bands whom performed for their avid followers. He sourced this information from Pastor Maxwell. The door stood partly open, and he could see what was going on within the Church with the bizarre Pastor Maxwell. He could faintly hear speaking and chanting, involving surreal words.

As he ventured closer, he could hear much more clearly. Alarm bells rang in Simon's mind. People were speaking the name he had discovered with Jennie. The 'Sanctuary of the Red Sun'. He was onto something. For once he neared the right answers he had been looking for. Simon questioned why the Sanctuary and these people had something to do with Isabelle's disappearance and killing. He crept closer to the side door, better able to see exactly what they were doing inside the Church. They wore special gowns and heavy brass neck chains that looked like talismans. Simon had seen these kinds of accessories a while back, during his psychic awareness training. Talismans were known throughout history to contain certain magical properties for achieving certain wishes, positivity, and good luck whilst attaining some kind of gain. To Simon's astonishment, he recalled these magical tools from a very long time ago-a time he had been much closer to himself and his beloved family. Daylight closed in while he observed the meeting, so Simon quickly jotted on his notepad the kind of garments they wore and the type of talismans around their sunken necks like golden lead weights. He felt a little panic within and a dire frustration. He put the pad back into his pocket and listened to the conversation between Pastor Maxwell and his gatherers.

The Pastor said,

'We are so much closer, my brethren, of forever light. We have almost accomplished what we set out to do, and you should be very proud of your gains during these times.'

The pastor gazed at his kneeled followers in front of the altar. One of the members angrily responded,

'We shouldn't have hurt those innocent people, Master.'

Alarmed and baffled, Simon remembered earlier research about the S.R.S. Their leader was known as the Master of the Sphinx, a legacy which went back hundreds of years. Utterly amazed, he let nothing distract him as the Master of the Sphinx began to speak to his secret group of devout followers.

'Our legacy goes back years, as you may well know; but it was tragic what happened to those people with purity through their eyes. They have something delicate and special to us which we need belongs to us, and you lot should know that!'

The Master of the Sphinx carried on addressing his sect,

'We hold much power now. We will gain full strength, dear brethren. You have shown your wisdom and courage under damnation into finding your path through the chosen light, that is why people like Isabelle was excluded from life. She had the divination tool we needed most entirely, but we will succeed. Are you with me or against me?'

Simon felt his whole life drifting into a storm of turmoil and confusion. Isabelle had been subject to methods by the 'Sanctuary of the Red Sun'.

'You bastards! Why?' screamed Simon.

'Who's there?' called the Master.

Simon panicked and dashed around, heading towards the main street, he quickly tilted his head back and noticed the Sanctuary brethren were alarmed and they stood guard like a small army they resembled, but an army of sadistic worshippers seeking the darkest of knowledge.

CHAPTER TEN

The overwhelming circumstances became quite a shock. He certainly had not a moment to waste. Simon ran as fast he could, trying to find where the taxi had parked. The vehicle was nowhere to be seen.

A police officer stopped him.

'Hold on. Mister. I have to ask you a few questions.'

'Officer, I am in a rush.'

'I noticed you were. This won't take too long. I am Officer Nelson and I noticed you were in a hurry. You broke the law.'

'I am sorry. Officer Nelson.'

'Can you just give me a ticket and I can make my way out of here?

'I am afraid I have to take you down to the station for a statement,' replied the determined Officer Nelson.

'No! please let me go, Simon begged while the policeman cuffed him and placed him into the back of the police vehicle.

Officer Nelson began driving towards the main highway. Out the back window, Simon could see the Sanctuary followers smiling so cunningly and deviously.

'Do we have much further to go now, Officer?'

'Not too long now. A few minutes.'

Officer Nelson turned into a back street alleyway and accelerated.

'I think we are going the wrong way, Officer.' Said Simon. The car sped, and Simon gasped for air while feeling strangulated fear. The policeman slowed, making a much smoother ride down a village lane, which was surreal after the previous action-packed journey.

'I know this place. I know where we are!' said Simon like an excited boy.

The vehicle headed through Vengers Lane, the home of Lord Cobbingham, a very powerful man and Simon's ancestor. The only weakness Lord Cobbingham had was losing both eyes in a horrific accident.

'We are here. Cobbingham Estate. Your Great Uncle wants to see you urgently, Simon. Sorry about that a moment ago, but I had to disguise you from that organisation. Well, if you call it that. By the way I am Sebastian.'

'Nice to meet you, Sebastian.' Simon replied, relieved and shaking his head.

'Just walk up to the gates. On the left you will see a chain. Give it a yank and be careful of the six bloodhounds on guard. Your uncle doesn't trust anybody since the accident, but he shall tell you more when you see him. Let me remove those cuffs. Sorry about that.'

Simon walked towards the towering iron gates. Voices rose from the grounds of the picturesque estate. Simon always known about the strange entities which still resided there. Cobbingham Estate was initially built by Puerto Rican settlers then disastrously burnt to the ground by Plantation Pirates whom received more than their greed afterwards. The sky began to crumble with quickening thunder. The sudden trembling movement of rain had the screaming hounds hypnotised and transfixed while gazing into thin air and avoiding their hourly guarding duties.

Simon pulled once at the iron chain. It was considerably tough to make a sound. A minute passed then a loud gong noise sent shudders through his already nervously shaking hand. Soon followed a screeching sound opposite from where he stood. A frail-looking man approached, a veteran of strength, yet with an antiquity of knowledge. He wore a black masonic uniform and Simon recognised him his ancestor, Lord Alfred Cobbingham. He had made many friends and enemies in his life, not surprisingly for a man with many religious and mysterious beliefs. He was once a thirty-third degree ranking freemason.

'Hello there, dear boy. It's your Uncle Alfred. Ignore the wires I have here on this horrid chair'

'Hello, Uncle'

Simon bowed to greet his honourable relative while stunned to see his horrific condition.

'Do you like the eye patches, dear boy? I had these from the mateys. You know. Pirates.'

'Ha-ha. You are still humorous. dear Uncle.' Simon chuckled.

'Come inside, dear boy. Sophia! Prepare lunch and fetch some of the finest brandy for my dear nephew and me,' called Lord Alfred.

'I have so much to speak to you about, dear nephew. Oh. Excuse my appearance.' Uncle Alfred fidgeting in his uniform jacket pocket.

'I have something of importance to show you, dear boy. Follow me.'

Lord Alfred rolled along on his wheelchair straight into the entrance door of his residence. The chair appeared as if it came from a futuristic movie. A sensor was implanted into Alfred's brain, more of a remote control sensor to detect what direction he would manoeuvre his seated transportation chair.

'The quickest thought, for the quickest direction, dear boy.' Said Alfred. He laughed excitingly.

'Reminds me of the magick.'

'I'll meet you in my library, dear boy. The last door on the left at the end of the corridor. See you shortly.' Alfred rolled away.

Bewildered, Simon softly strolled along the hallway's grandeur. Simon observed several artefacts and family heirlooms upon the walls as he walked along the corridor. A rare grin appeared on his face as he reminisced about a special childhood moment in his parent's involvement with various spiritual science groups. He never had the comfort of family sitting around the table at dinner. The usual nanny would be called upon on a weekly basis while his mother and father would sneak outside in the dead of night to visit their hidden magical abode. Something caught Simon's eye. Immediately he went to a cabinet on the far wall. It was similar to a museum display counter. He glanced over his shoulder, and since nobody was about, he unlocked this cabinet to retrieve the illuminated item.

'Put that down, boy!'

His Uncle Lord Alfred fumed while racing his chair along the corridor.

'I don't recognise this, Uncle?' said Simon, curiously.

'That item belonged to your Great Aunty Agatha. It has been in the family for many years. Much history, you can say, about that wand you were holding, and please do not touch anything else!'

Uncle Alfred reached into his left pocket and fetched a hankie to wipe sweat from his brow. Simon recalled that Alfred enjoyed speaking about history and many stories, and especially now, he rarely had any visitors. The last guest had been shot at. Uncle Alfred never liked rude people, so he chased him out of the estate with his antique colt and fired rounds of bullets into the visitor's backside. He certainly never returned to Cobbingham after that event. Simon followed his Uncle down the corridor to the study room.

'Sit down, dear boy,' said Lord Alfred whilst plucking at his dust- filled moustache.

He had a slight resemblance of an old buccaneer without the rum.

'Coffee or a Twining's tea? What would you prefer, dear boy?'

'I will have a strong coffee please, dear Uncle'

'Do you think this is Brazil, dear boy? Ha-ha!' joked Uncle Alfred.

'Sophia. Sophia!' called Alfred to his servant.

They waited like estranged mice awaiting their beverages to arrive from Sophia.

'I see how you look at her, Uncle Alfred'

'Who?'

'The way you drool over Sophia.' Replied Simon.

Sophia finally arrived with their drinks. Alfred accepted his and slapped Sophia's bottom as she walked with a giggle. She headed to the kitchen for preparation for dinner. Simon couldn't hide his amazed expression after witnessing his Uncle Alfred's style of honest humour.

'I have always been a bottom man, dear boy. Ha-ha!' declared Uncle Alfred with a loud laugh.

'Enough hanky panky. Let me tell you why you are here. I will -

-tell you what you have always wanted to hear, but didn't know.' Said Alfred with a serious look while staring through into Simon's psychic eyes.

They were both staring directly at each other to Simon's great curiosity. No sound could be heard. No movement. Only the stillness of the hypnotising ornamental glare and the clicking sound of the 'Newton's cradle' resting on the mahogany gramophone cabinet. What would be told? What could possibly be such an important revelation? Should a new discovery be made, what would be unravelled at this moment?

CHAPTER ELEVEN

Alfred reached under the cushion of his leather-bound wheelchair and handed Simon what appeared to be a parchment scroll wrapped with a worn out waxed leather cord in the shape of a coiled two-headed serpent. Maybe this would hold more clues into Isabelle's tragic death? Simon didn't utter a single word as he became transfixed by what he held within his grasp.

'This seems to be years old, Uncle.'
'Don't open it just yet, dear boy. You will know when the time shall be. Do you understand?' said Alfred while clenching his hands onto the chair.

Alfred began to tell Simon the reason why he was driven to see him at his estate, but as Alfred began to speak a crashing sound sent vibrations through the hallway to the study room. An intruder alert signalled through to Uncle Alfred's wheelchair, and the noise came from the iron entrance gates.
'Oh, no!' Simon stood.
'We have to get out of here now. Take that scroll with you and keep it safe,' Alfred instructed as they made a hasty escape.
'Quickly, Simon, I'll tell you something quickly. My eyes were-

-taken out by the 'Sanctuary' and Jennie and Jack aren't the people you think they are. Now go! Get out of here. There is a tunnel under the kitchen floor, and look for the sign. Now go!' said Alfred while trying to keep guard of his blessed fortune of Cobbingham estate.

Simon scuffled like a wolf in the kitchen. Uncle Alfred had something about a 'sign', so Simon followed along the chequered marbled floor. He noticed a sequence of black and white squares, but the pattern began to follow with a red square formation. He had to work out a mathematical code to figure where the clue was hiding. He began to realise that maybe it was a calendar date, and suddenly he remembered a date, the date his Uncle Alfred took possession of the private Cobbingham estate. It was surreal that the day Alfred had signed the property agreement was on the sixth day of the sixth month and the sixth hour. **666**.

The bible recognises this number in revelations as the number or mark of the beast. Could Uncle Alfred really be a beast, or a man of dark tendencies? A frail old man who couldn't see with his own two eyes, but had a sixth sense about his surroundings, including women. Simon found a kitchen ladle, an ideal tool to loosen the sixth floor tile. The hacking tool sent painful vibrations from his fingers to his upper arm as sweat began to pour from his throbbing forehead. The clock was ticking, and he needed to hurry on out of there. When he finally pried the tiles away, he found a pole leading into the depths. It didn't take long for him to slither the pole, even though he had to pass through numerous spider webs and stenches. Underneath the estate, Simon entered a passageway, Uncle Alfred previously told him that it was once used by smugglers and heretic preachers avoiding execution. The swamped floor was tiring with drips of sewage splashing into a nearby disused underground rail track.

He could hear the echoes of the dead souls who had died within this hallowed underground passage. The humid air and dampness was overbearing, and he shuffled through his pocket for his medication as he tramped through the filthy stained pathway alongside the rail track. He almost felt the need to pass out due to the lack of air and the staleness from pollution. The end of the disused track led outside into the new Cobbingham vineyard only recently constructed. A tumbling metallic sound rang in Simon's ears. This sound become much louder. He looked around like a scavenging canine. A rail cart headed his way, and he panicked. He started running and leapt like a hunted fox. A voice followed in the distance with a crackling portrayal of laughter. Simon was in shock to recognise his manager's laugh. How had Jack gotten there? Simon finally exited the underground with a whirlwind of thoughts. He raced through the orchard adjacent to the building. Dehydration got the better of him, and he slowly drifted to the ground within the vineyard with the sound of the painful cries of Uncle Alfred's voice in the distance. Simon quickly undressed and washed his clothing in a nearby stream to rid it of the horrid stench from sewage and decay that had fouled the passageway. While cleansing his pants and shirt, he could see his manager and members of the 'Sanctuary' had his uncle. Alfred kept many medieval relics, including torture instruments. Simon was traumatised to see they had seated his uncle upon a wooden pyramid-like structure known as the 'Judas Chair'.

During the medieval period, prisoners were stripped naked and humiliated whilst forced to sit upon the chair with the sharp pyramid point inserted into their anus and genital area. Weights were placed at either side of the victim to inflict the worst kind of pain and agony as they danced to the terror of death and the approaching eternal life. Terrified, Simon could see Alfred seated upon this device and the colour of crimson streaming down to the trembling tips of his aged toes. His bloated stomach filled with suffering death until Uncle Alfred gasped for his last gorged breath. Flocks of birds appeared over Simon's head then flew for a delicate feast of Alfred's corpse. The smell of blood was immense. Simon felt nauseous and was upset. He quickly dressed in his now heavy and dampened clothes. His uncle had a garage with some of the most valuable motorbikes and cars. He would head that way. Gallantly shifting through the vineyard marshland and avoiding any possible witnesses, Simon climbed down a hatch at the side of the garage. It was a tight squeeze, even for a man of his lean structure. Wrestling with blankets of dusted cobwebs, he spiralled down the enclosed hatch. He sneaked his way through the grasslands, avoiding any possible sight from the nearby sanctuary members and Jack. He crawled through thick terrain as a storm front arrived. The sky emulsified with a pitch black vaporing mist of thunderous shadows. The ground began to sink, and Simon struggled with anxiousness and panic while he tried to shift along through the now swamped land. A heavy foot came out of nowhere, sending Simon into a hazed state of mind. He passed out momentously, then gazed up at where Jack stood over him, disguised in a black robe. That hideous laughter soon followed as dragged him along the dirt swamped marshlands to Cobbingham Estate. Laughter grew much louder as they neared. Spitting dried soil from his aching, blood-stained teeth, Simon heard the sound of Gregorian chants. He struggled to free himself from the clutches of Jack. Four 'Sanctuary' members now man handled Simon. They threw him into a vehicle with blackened windows then urinated upon his back. The stench had a thickening scent.

'Get off me now!' Simon shouted.

'You thought you could get away, didn't you?' replied the cloaked sanctuary member.

They tied his hands and arms together, the resin of rope cutting deeply into his pained wrists. Simon fidgeted like a slithering worm with anticipation of setting himself free. Within moments of forcing a way out of the restrained knots, blood from his deluged wounds flew into the air like a shimmering flight of birds from a red sea. Blood softly soaked the interior of the vehicle, disguising the cloaked sanctuary members with a haze of illuminated crimson. Music still poured through speakers, which were adjusted louder by a female sitting in the driver seat. That irritating laughter came back. Jennie sat back in a sexual seated position as she revealed her parted legs to Simon, exposing her vagina as she sat wearing a dark cloak like the others. The exposed pale moon skin and her fruited breasts teased Simon, he became disorientated furthermore when Jennie applied Chanel lipstick, she grinned devilishly. Jennie puckered her lips at Simon as she stood up from the seat and wriggled her milk-white flesh at him. He couldn't believe what an evil bitch she really was. She giggled nightmarishly, leaning forward and lifting up the black robe from her rear. Still targeting her fiery eyes at him, she began to utter some words.

'Want to fuck me like your uncle and father did, Simon?'

Jennie sat back down while she threw her cloak at him. She now only wore a smile dressed in a paint of blood from Simon's wounds. The opposite door opened, and Jack sat down alongside

Jennie.

'Are you at ease there, Simon?' asked Jack with humour.

Simon's eyes fluttered with mental pictures of betrayal and confusion, and his ears throbbed thunderously with the haunting chant music which still flowed from the speakers.

'We shall begin very soon,' said Jennie.

Her voice hitching on an excited note as she drove. The engine revved up slowly, gathering speed with the crunching sound of tyres pulling through the dirt road, and spraying debris onto the nearby hedgerows. Jennie was an impatient driver. She never wanted to miss an opportunity to be mischievous. She drove to the pedestrian subway entrance. It looked impossible to control the steering wheel while she screamed insanely.

'We are almost at Jerusalem Lodge, everyone' said Jack abruptly.

One of the members replied back nervously,

'Do we have what we need?'

'We shall have everything, my friend,' replied Jack while clenching his hands together with a devious grin.

Finally, the wagon pulled along a side street next to the lodge. The weather had drastically changed even more. Amidst the frequent rain and greyness of scattered clouds, it began to thunder. Figures of dark shadows crept from the wagon to the side entrance of Jerusalem Lodge. The calling of crows sitting upon spires high above the building sent atmospheric shivers. Simon, on the other hand, was at his weakest point of desperation. Cold humidity from the stormy weather created a rising mist from the cobbled path. Lodge members placed a black sack over Simon's head. He felt suffocated and lost. His heart began to beat faster as they dragged him out of the wagon. He didn't have any clue where they were taking him. He tried to focus on happy times with his beloved, but he was so distraught and empty while becoming weaker, as if his psychic energies were escaping his body into the night sky. A door slammed behind him. The air was enclosed with a muted silence. Not even a sound of dripping water could be heard. An organ being played in the distance. It echoed a melodic haunt, sending Simon's secluded thoughts into a crazier direction. The increasing sound of footsteps soon followed. They began to move at a quickened pace, then suddenly stopped. A door creaked open.

Simon Finally had the black bag taken from his head. Was he in some kind of magical temple? Surrounding walls held artefacts which seemed of a rare antiquity, many in an Egyptian style. Placed in the centre of the floor was a table which looked different. A 'Sanctuary' member knelt in front of the table while chanting words of a summoning nature:

Teach me, O creator of all things, to have correct knowledge and understanding, for your wisdom is all that I desire. Speak your word in my ear, O creator of all things, and set your wisdom in my heart.

There were five rooms in two rows facing each other. Simon recognised this lodge as long lost memories suddenly came flooding back. It was like a mental curtain opened to reveal the unknown. He was now led into another room by the Master of the Sphinx while delivering commanding words to him.

'Now it's your turn to deliver and summon with us,' said the master. He gulped, secluded into a dark and strangulated realisation. They wanted his psychic abilities to bring forth a series of demonic spirits. Nothing like this had been attempted by anyone in many years.

'I can't do this!' Simon yelled.

The master and other 'Sanctuary' members came into the room and struck Simon's face and body with punches. He screamed in agonising pain. When they eventually left, they slammed the door. Simon was now lost in a darkened room of mystical surroundings. His mind felt heavy and swollen. He didn't know how to escape from this abysmal building. Mirrors hung like hidden boxes from mosaicked walls. He thought he could hear trapped souls within the isolation. Memoirs of unknowing, sort of foreign from the outside world, came to Simon's senses. A large table stood in the centre of the reflecting floor. He saw the floor was also tainted like a glass. It looked like a black obsidian mirrored flooring. He needed to go to the holy table, mere yards for his aching, blood soaked shoes to walk. He heaved his exhausted body from the floor and slowly headed towards the table. He remembered he had the scroll, which he had retrieved from the wagon while being held captive. He quickly pulled the scroll from his pocket and unrolled the old parchment tied with a waxed ribbon. Its letterings he recognised from the Enochian alphabet, but many scholars call it the 'Language of the Angels'. Simon knew he had to perform this hand-written ritual. Not even a message was included in the scroll, just a lesson on salvation of oneself. This reading must have been many centuries old, but of great importance to the outer limits of other worldly realms. He could taste dry ash smoke from burning incense, which was fumigating the mirrored room. Time was counting like a doomsday clock.

Simon sat in front of the table, trying not to be distracted by the walls of embedded darkness within these mirrors and avoiding staring into the reflective blackened floor. He began to read the Enochian scroll while a ring and lamen appeared attached to the left side of the ritual paper. He knew this to be the ring of Babylon and the seal of Agorum, and he had to wear these to complete the summoning. Simon started to calmly chant the words of wisdom,

Behold the Ring, Lo, this it is. This is it, wherewith all miracles and divine works and wonders were wrought by Solomon: this is it, which the Archangel Michael has revealed to me. This is it, which Philosophy dreameth of. This is it, which the Angels scarce know. This is it, and blessed be his name: yea, his name be blessed forever. Without this I shall do nothing. Blessed be his name, that encompasses all things. Wonders are in him, and his name is WONDERFUL: PELE. His name works wonders from generation to generation. Amen.

He gazed spiritually, without a thought of negativity. He had to be strong to hold a positive karma. He stared at the magical holy table and began to chant more words.

Behold the Lamen. As the Holy Table conciliates Heaven and Earth, let this Lamen which I place over my heart conciliate me to the Holy Table. Amen.

There was something missing. He needed a wand, but he had to improvise quickly. He discovered broken twigs in his pockets from earlier when 'Sanctuary' brethren had dragged him through the marshlands. It was perfect. He continued reading and chanting the scroll. He chose one of the twigs and held the makeshift wand. He reached across the holy table, tapping the upper right-hand corner, and began to chant while moving the tip of the wand from right to left along the far edge of the table and chanting more.

Pa Med Fam Med Drux Fam Fam Ur Ged Graph Drux Med Graph Graph Med Med Or Med Gal Ged Ged Drux

Simon then moved the tip of the wand down the left edge of the table, continuing to chant.

Pa Drux Un Tal Fam Don Ur Graph Don Or Gisg Gon Med Un Ged Med Graph Van Ur Don Don Un.

He continued the experimental practice and moved the wand from left to right along the bottom edge of the table.

Pa Drux Ur Ur Don Ur Drux Un Med Graph Graph Med Med Graph Ceph Ged Ged Ur Mais Mais Fam Un

Gradually, he glided the twig-made wand further up the right hand side of the table to finish where he started.

Pa Gon Med Un Graph Fam Mais Tal Ur Pa Pa Drux Un Un Van Un Med Un Gon Drux Drux I Ir.

He's repeated this several more times, each time with increased intensity and focus on the words and movements. Finally, he completed this stage of chanting.

Now he had to attend to several other verses of Enochian chants.

Med Gon Gisg, Don Ur Van, Ur Don Ur, Med Med Graph. Med Don Ur Med, Gon Ur Don Med, Gisg Van Ur Graph.

Simon approached a state of trance.

He had to trace a circle with the wand over the centre of the table and call out these words with the names of the archangels.

Seven, rest in Seven, and the Seven, live by Seven, The Seven, govern the Seven, and by Seven all Government is.
Galas Gethog Thaoth Horlum Innon Aaoth Galethog,
Zaphkiel Zedekiel Cumael Raphael Haniel Michael Gabriel,
Me Esc Iana Akele Azdobon Stimcul
I Ih Ilr Dmal Heeoa Beigia Stimcul,
S Ab Ath Izad Ekiei Madimi Esemeli,
E An Ave Liba Rocle Hagonel Hemes,
Sabathiel Zadkiel Madimiel Semeliel Nogahel Corabiel
Lavanael

Soon after, Simon placed the wand over the centre of his forehead and softly whispered.

luah lang sach urch
lad mo/ zir—iad bab zna—iad sor gru—iad ser osf.

Several moments passed with Simon in an altered state of consciousness. He felt incredibly high and lifeless, drifting into an atmospheric daze. He stood up from his cramped, seated position and fell against the black obsidian mirror on the left side of the wall. He was also trying to recover from dehydration and from being high. His shivered breath steamed the mirror. Screeching vibrations began to touch and echo through Simon's now vivid senses while his face was magnetised against the taunting mirror. He slowly rotated his head and flickered his confused eyes open. He shouted to the mirror,
'Does this have to happen to me? What the fuck have I done to you?'
Voices from the past haunted his postcard mentality like an etched memoir from the Devil. His mind tumbled into an uncontrollable realm of formidable darkness. The worst dreams Simon once had, simultaneously came flooding back this instant. During each minute that passed, he become more delirious and confused, tormented with visuals of illuminated spectrums from angelic realms. He wasn't sure whether he wanted to die, but he didn't

know who he was or where he was. Time passed, and Simon felt sedated like a mental patient upon the floor. He was in a prolonged dream, a spiritual curse which had now be open into the modern world. There was only method of resolving his awakening and restoring his psychic abilities. It would require a prism-like object called 'The Mind's Eye'. If this object was in the wrong hands, an unimaginable, controllable, hypnotising event would soon follow. 'The Mind's Eye' had the power to feed from human thought and consume the most powerful secrets.

Taken from the forthcoming anthology

Doomsday *after* Midnight

Available 2015

The Gathering

The time was almost close to the midnight hour when the train travelling back from Fairlight Haven was due to arrive thirty minutes ahead of the designated schedule from the dreary mute village of Halford Manor. The most peculiar look appeared on the face of Charles Davenport. He had this thick combed moustache of a darkened black colour and he never departed his residence without an immaculate appearance. He was an old fashioned romantic when it came to the female species and when Charles was a young boy he witnessed something which would have much effect on him during his present life. Charles is a man of almost seven foot tall and he decided to wear his best double breasted black pinstripe suit for this particular day. He felt slightly uncomfortable because the last time he wore that suit was at the Wedding to his beloved wife Charlotte. Momentarily the expression upon Charles Davenport's face quickly appeared withdrawn and lost, reminiscing of how life previously was. The signal bells across the train platform were shattering with the most intense sound as the train was about to finally appear.

The morning frosted mist was thickening in an array of grey clouds while the calling of a bird sitting perched upon the upper clock face tower looked mystifying and alert to the movements of Mr Davenport. He picked up his typewriter case from the waiting area of the platform and boarded the train to Elsworth Castle. The shattering sound of the cabin doors were beginning to annoy

Charles as he was searching for room number 13. He quickly grabbed his case and walked down the cabin corridor and finally came to the entrance of cabin 13. He felt an ease of contentment, as it was his first time to relax in many months, due to the work Mr Davenport was involved with, and this work had a substantial meaning to Charles. Nobody knew or recalled that terrible day, the day Charlotte died. Charlotte was adored by many of the local townspeople; they could see she had issues which she kept well hidden. Issues which were a vision like no other. She was immaculately beautiful whilst wearing an angelic smile, a smile quite calming like the soothing breeze of day, but the hellish storm soon faded her away into darkness. Charles just woken from a deserved rest and he can still see clearly the image of the stillness upon the face of Charlotte, her face of a porcelain paleness white was painted with a terrifying picture of death and soaked crimson tears. He gazed with his dreary tired eyes looking out of the cabin window. His whispered breath painted a reflective image of sadness upon the glass. Those last words of hearing the screams of his beloved Charlotte, but a grin suddenly appeared upon Mr Davenport's cunning and devious pose of expression.

He stared at the picturesque view of the mountain range from within his cabin. A scientific thought of an uplifting cleanse appeared to him, he quickly looked at the time on his pocket clock and realized to himself he had to make certain required notes of what he was about to do within his special experimentation procedure. An hour passed into the journey aboard the train to Elsworth Castle. Several weeks passed by so quickly since he was last in the marital home of his rural abode. The strangest feeling happened almost suddenly as if the train was filled with emptiness, no passengers were travelling, or to be seated but only Mr Davenport. Usually this train is at the busiest time of year with commuters. The final whistle soon came to alert the destination for the village of Elsworth. Charles collected his typewriter case and departed the train. The fresh country air gave a moment of relief as Charles looked around and realized he was home. The stagecoach was waiting at the right side of the station in the darkness of the cobbled stoned alleyway.

The stench of rotting meat and the sound of rats were irritating and painful to delicate ears, which Charles had a severe ear infection as a child, whilst undergoing various horrid treatments, such as blood sucking leeches in the ear to heal the suffering. Charles dashed to the alleyway while looking deviously scared as he stepped into the black horse shaped stagecoach as the illuminated carriage appeared lonesome with only Samuel Butterfield as the Chauffeur.

'Good day to you Master Charles' said Mr Butterfield as he bowed

'Hello dear boy we better get a move on. Great things are coming our way! ' replied Mr Davenport excitingly

'Yes Sir' replied Samuel with a cunning shyness.

It has been a life changing time for Samuel Butterfield. He was a short round boy whom was neglected as an infant for being born with a disfigurement due to a growth disorder. His parents owned a circus and trained timid animals and turned them into wild beasts. 'Pug face' was a name he was tormented with throughout his youth while frequently bullied and tortured by his parents. Most children slept in the comfort in their beds at night, but Samuel had the worst nightmare of sleeping outside within the dampness in the dog kennels, whilst surviving on the scraps of suffered animal carcasses.

'I still see those dogs Master! ' said Samuel while choking emotionally

'Did you have your medicine dear boy? 'Replied a concerned Mr Davenport

'Do I have to Master? Replied Samuel Butterfield frightfully

'Yes you do! Now take it and don't be a pug face! 'Said Master Charles angrily

Samuel began to cry and shiver resembling a little lost child in the woods from the remark from his keeper, Master Charles. But Samuel knew he dare to not answer back, he had to follow strict orders and who knows how life would have been without being rescued by Master Charles?

Life finally changed for the better in that bleak period when Charles found Samuel sitting on the steps of his cold and distant country palace. Mr Davenport always wanted a Son, but since

Charlotte's incident that dream became impossible, a vivid dream of emotions it surely was to be endured. The moment arrived as the painted black carriage pulled up alongside the entrance path to Elsworth Castle. The empty grey sky opened up with a sea of swollen clouds and the flickering shadows of approaching black Ravens in a flight of desperation towards the Castle. Charles and Samuel dragged their worn out feet up the blistering path as humid rain began to melt from the surfacing blackening sky. The smell of burnt ash filled the Castle entrance with a blinded fog. Samuel sunk his hand into the heaviness of his pocket to retrieve the door key. After entering through the large framed doors the musical chime of Charlotte's music box began to play repeatedly. The dullness of the main hall was nothing more than a theatrical ambience. The walls were painted red with an overlook of a vast amount of ancestry portraits; it was as if the walls had watchful eyes. Samuel Butterfield never liked this room, but for Charles Davenport this was his haven.

Next to the main hall was a room which still was securely locked since Charles embarked on his studies. Mr Davenport named this The Gathering Room. If visitors were invited as guests there were shown the beauty and art surrounding the walls within this secret room. But moments before guests arrived, the stench was intensifying with the lingering smell of fear and distant screams of death lurking behind every picture painted smile.

The day was too much for Mr Davenport, he had to rest for an early morning of science. The following morning Samuel Butterfield collected the invitational telegrams from the postal office at the local village for an evening's show of dinner and dance. Charles was unaware of what was about to happen later on this day. Mr Davenport woken from his night of rest and the sound of the music box began playing over and over again. A message of melody and emotion appeared on the face of Charles just as he began to tweak the hair of his moustache. The last time he heard the music box orchestrating to his inner thoughts was the day poor Charlotte died. He couldn't live and deal with this pain no longer and had to miraculously use his knowledge of scientific thought to achieve something so much greater than he ever did.

Life was a distant dream, but Charles wanted his dream to

become a living reality once more. To relive the beauty and innocence of his poor lost love. If only he could feel her and have her so close once more, nothing else would matter. Samuel arrived back to Elsworth Castle for the preparation for the evening party. The guest list included several local important figures, such as Tradesmen and Actresses whom were close to Charles's wife Charlotte and they would have done anything for her, but couldn't even acknowledge her suffering during that dreadful day of her sudden death. Charlotte was social with everyone except Samuel Butterfield. She felt neglected by her Husband when he took in that cold little disfigured boy from that step on that shallow bitter day. Jealousy finally became her companion and broke her heart with fits of rage and bullying towards Samuel. One day, Samuel could not take this anymore; the painful antics had to quickly fade. Mr Davenport had his own laboratory with the most equipped chemicals and medical tools for the cure of disease.

Samuel went over to the cabinet and pulled the weighted bottle of acid while quickly hiding it under his Butler apron to deliver Charlotte her morning tea. As he approached the bedroom of the Davenport's, he waited timidly by the lover's room, as soon as he heard Charles enter the en-suite bathroom he lifted the bottle from his jacket and splashed the chemical upon the angelic face of pretty Charlotte. The acid melted away her innocence and smile, revealing nothing more than an ongoing vision of beauty which once was. She couldn't live with her monstrous appearance, just as Charles came back from the bathroom he noticed the window was wide open and the cotton white curtains were blowing with the morning breeze with the sound of the music box playing, but Charlotte wasn't to be seen. She leapt to her death from window. Charles dashed to the curtain while the music box stopped playing. His beloved was faded into the darkness of the greyest of days, Charles never shown much emotion throughout his life; he always distracted his pain with the knowledge of achieving. Since that terrifying day, Charles focused vigorously into gaining the most advanced knowledge known to man and existence.

He worked as a Doctor at the Burntwood Asylum while gaining a better understanding to human emotional suffering. They tried to commit Charles on two occasions for the infliction of pain towards his patients. But the eyes of Mr Davenport you could see he was pleasured insanely. The thrill he gained from defenseless victims whilst in the care of his tormented and greedy hands.

The present day, Samuel and Charles had to get preparations in order for when the Guests arrived to dine and welcome back home Charles Davenport. He headed to his Laboratory to find something special to acquire towards a seasoning for the main course meals of that night. Charles hysterically overcame with excitement as he approached the further end of the lab, with another hidden room.

There were several large metallic tables in rows of three, shelving with jars filled with various frightening species of human and non-human parts, including a two -headed baby. But Charles was after something more of a delicacy for the guests of his honoured presence. He noticed a collection of Dermestidae, also known as 'skin beetles'. The arousing delightful thought reached out with amusement from the mind of Charles. Once these insects touched human skin they would instantly crack into the skin of its victim and deliver the most excruciating pain and sudden flesh eating death. He didn't care about these guests, the only person he cared for was his dear Charlotte, and to Charles it was there fault and they should suffer dire consequences.

The time of seven o 'clock soon arrived and guests began to gather downstairs in the drawing room across from the main hall. The irritating laughter was eccentric and annoyed both Charles and Samuel. Charles was standing at the top of the spiral staircase looking down towards his devious disciples. Samuel Butterfield on the other hand was sniggering away mischievously near the seating area where the guests were waiting. Mr Davenport began a formal speech under the shadow with the reflection of evil appearing from the lavish décor on the staircase wall. The glowing light of the spinning chandelier flickering from the stillness of those vengeful piercing eyes which Samuel feared so dearly.

'Thank you all for coming to this wonderful evening, without you I would not have been here today smiling and feeling proud, so please relax and help yourself to the drinks in the main hall'

Said Charles has he just bowed with a sign of a fulfilling relief.

'Samuel can you fetch me the Paraldehyde, it is located in the second cabinet in my Laboratory' hesitantly stated Master Charles

'Yes Master', replied Samuel as he nervously collected the item.

Samuel quickly strolled down the echoing corridor to Mr Davenport's Laboratory. Paraldehyde' is known as a hypnotic sedative which can cause the most advance illusions or nightmares to make appearance from a person's mind. Mr Davenport had a vast knowledge of these medicinal uses and terms while studying at the criminally insane Asylum and the affects which they can do were to be out of this world.

Samuel gathered the liquid drug and headed towards the cellar and handed over the deadly ingredient to Master Charles while his expression became motionless and faint at the thought of this evenings devastating attraction.

Charles began to mumble.

'We shall have peace my dear Charlotte, they won't know what surprises await them, and we shall succeed'

Charles began to jump excitingly like a crazed lunatic and clap his hands. The guests finally were seated for their dinner serving; elsewhere in the kitchen Samuel added the drug to the beef gravy which was to accompany the beef wellington dish. Master Charles on the other hand was clenching the jar of skin beetles, usually the infested insects would be hyper-active and hungry, but luckily for Charles he was an important man on a killing mission and moments before he inserted a temporary gas to the jar to calm the activity of the flesh eating bugs. Samuel finally began to walk with an expression like a waiter from hell clenching at the tray carrying the hallucinogenic concoction. As he approached the dinner table, the reaping countdown had begun. The guests were becoming hungry and impatient for the arrival of dinner. They began to dip Italian breadsticks into the gravy. Moments later, one of the guests looked across the table and could see fairies dancing behind another seated guest's chair. The most peculiar expression appeared on their faces.

The meal was almost ready; Charles turned upside down and emptied the beetles under the pastry layer of the beef wellington surprise dish. Samuel delivered the frightful feast of beef wellington and placed a portion upon the guest's plates. Silence entered the dinner hall; some guests were acting disorderly, while others were in a state of an uncomforting trance. The visitors appeared dead and lost within each and every one of them. They were still alive, but under a quickness of an ornamented hypnotised pose. Samuel began to force fed each of the guests and chanting out rhymes while limping towards the next ill-fated casualty. The night soon faded into an overpowering evening of shadowed anguished death. Once were breathing guests, soon became dinner dates of the devil. Charles acted quickly, he ran towards his Laboratory to retrieve his implements for what he was about to do. He needed skin, enough skin to paint his walls of picturesque beauty. He believed beauty was skin deep. He knew that by using these beetles the skin of his helpless victims would still be freshly intact.

'Decisions, decisions, incisions' said Charles as he screamed aloud with enjoyment!

Charles had the sharpest knife in one hand and surgical scissors in the other and glided himself across the killing floor. Later that evening, Elsworth Castle felt much more like a home. The fires were burning; the surroundings seemed like a forgotten dream. Charles was feeling proud at his new exhibit within the gathering room. A cunning devious expression appeared on the face of Mr Davenport while looking at the wall of souls, a new exhibition like no other, Samuel was close by, even closer to Mr Davenport. He always admired a new chair from a special man made leather. The music box played as Charles stared directly at his beloved Charlotte; it was the prettiest music box he has ever owned.

ABOUT THE AUTHOR

Anthony Crowley (born 1979, Birmingham in U.K). From a young age, Anthony began to take an interest in English literature and poetry from early childhood. Then throughout his teenage years he studied music and developed his song-writing skills, whilst still creating his visions. He also achieved a diploma in creative writing with a college located in Oxford, England. Anthony has also written short stories for student newsletters and horror monthlies. In the present day Anthony Crowley is a featured contributor to *'Haunted after Dark'* with his very own dark haven of 'Crowley's Crypt' and has written many works of literature & poetry for publications, such as, *Massacre Magazine, Sanitarium, HelloHorror*. The dark verse of *'The Fallen Angel'* featured in *Sanitarium Magazine* issue 14. The work itself was mentioned via a live radio podcast on the evening of Halloween 2013.

'The Devils Foot Soldier' was another dark verse which was inspired by the *Slasher Icon* movie of 2011 *The Orphan Killer* which was positively recognized by the movie's creators and the written piece is now featured at US-based *Blood Born Magazine*. He is highlighted in several more features and frequent media interviews and being ranked as "one of the best Modern Authors in recent years". Horror-Web described him with the following statement 'Anthony Crowley is one of the most prolific and talented authors of dark prose and poetry'.

During a recent interview on *Sinister Scribblings* Mr Crowley has been placed amongst the likes of Poe, Lovecraft and Clarke Ashton Smith. Forthcoming Novella *The Mirrored Room* was ranked in the semi-finals in the 'AuthorsdB' Book Awards of 2013,and ranked four times in the 'Top 100' list of popular authors, not forgetting that he was a trending author for many consecutive months and a featured author on numerous literature and horror-themed websites and more.

Presently, Anthony Crowley has published the best-selling horror anthology *Tombstones* and the introduction to a new dark series *The Black Diaries*.

Anthony Crowley dubbed "the Master of Realities" is always creating new and exciting projects within the genres of speculative literature and Horror, Occult and Historic references.. Anthony is currently resides in England

ANTHONY CROWLEY
BIBLIOGRAPHY

The Black Diaries (Volume One) – *A collection of short Horror themed fiction & dark poetic verse literature*, including; The Conjuring Road and Ghost & the Raven

Available from all good book stockists, *including* Amazon & Barnes and Noble
Also available on Kindle

ISBN-10: 1497307759
ISBN-13: 978-1497307759

TOMBSTONES – *A collection of some of the finest dark verse literature whilst exploring the various elements of Horror, fear, emotions & the macabre*

Available from all good book stockists, *including* Amazon, Books-a-Million & Barnes and Noble

Also available on Kindle
Coming Soon to Audible audiobooks

ISBN-10: 1497552796
ISBN-13: 978-1497552791

Other Anthony Crowley works, including featured appearances in Sanitarium & Massacre Magazine, The Horror zine, visit
The Official Amazon stores –

www.amazon.com/ANTHONYCROWLEY/e/B0048E5L3K/

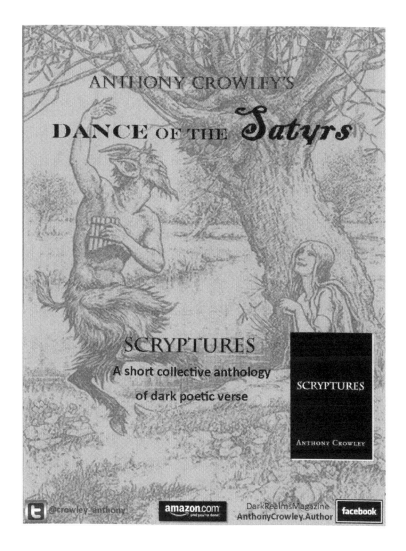

'HAVE YOU READ **HAUNTED AFTER DARK**?

Featuring Crowley's Crypt WITH YOUR HOST

ANTHONY CROWLEY

COMING SOON FROM ANTHONY CROWLEY

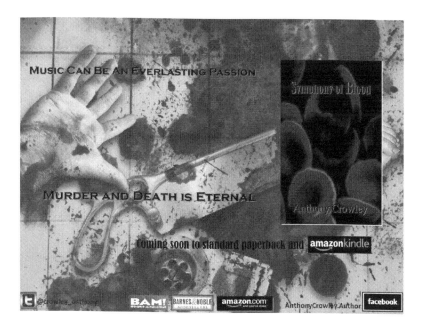

Check out the Official ANTHONY CROWLEY pages at-

TWITTER - @crowley_anthony

FACEBOOK- AnthonyCrowley.Author

INSTAGRAM- anthonycrowleyauthor

THE OFFICIAL **TOMBSTONES** PAGES

TWITTER- @TombstonesBook
FACEBOOK- TombstonesBook

- Clearly the editor of this book was not paying attention to detail as it is riddled with spelling errors.

- The story itself is utterly confusing with quiet the amount of incomplete thoughts and things mentioned out of the blue that really don't make sense.

Because of these facts I put the book down many times out of frustration and confusion.

It was difficult to remain focused.

Made in the USA
Lexington, KY
19 February 2015